Why a Disguise?

By Laura Numeroff

Illustrated by David McPhail

SIMON & SCHUSTER BOOKS FOR YOUNG READERS

SIMON & SCHUSTER BOOKS FOR YOUNG READERS An imprint of Simon & Schuster Children's Publishing Division
1230 Avenue of the Americas, New York, New York 10020. Text copyright © 1996 by Laura Numeroff. Illustrations copyright © 1996 by
David McPhail. All rights reserved including the right of reproduction in whole or in part in any form. SIMON & SCHUSTER BOOKS FOR
YOUNG READERS is a trademark of Simon & Schuster. Book design by Paul Zakris. The text of this book is set in 19-point Journal Ultra.
The illustrations are rendered in watercolor. Manufactured in the United States of America First Edition 10 9 8 7 6 5 4 3 2 1
LIBRARY OF CONGRESS CATALOGING-IN-PUBLICATION DATA
Numeroff, Laura Joffe.
Why a disguise? / by Laura Numeroff ; illustrated by David McPhail
p.   cm.
Summary: Relates how a disguise can be used to evade the school bully, Mom's lima beans, and other unpleasant things.
[1. Disguise—Fiction.   2. Identity—Fiction.]   I. McPhail, David M., ill.   II. Title.
PZ7.N964Wh   1996   [E]—dc20   93-19025   CIP AC   ISBN 0-689-80513-6

For Stephanie Owens Lurie and
Nick, Cathy, and Karl Taylor
—L. N.

For Ben Brink, ball player
—D. M.

A disguise is a very handy
thing to have around.

Wear it to the dentist's office.
Then the nurse won't say,
"It's your turn."

How *can* he if he doesn't think
you're in the waiting room?

Don't lend it to your sister.

She might put it on
when it's her turn
to set the table.

Then *you* will have to do it.

Do wear it when the school bully
says he's going to wait for you
after school!

Just make sure it doesn't fall off.

Put it on
when your moth
makes lima bear

She won't know it's you, so she
won't make you eat them.

A great time to put on your disguise
is when you have
to take a bath.

You might want to
add a different hat.

Put it on before your father comes into your room to tell you it's time to get ready for school.

Tell him the person he's
looking for has already left.

Remember to wear it
when relatives
come over.

Then they won't pinch your cheek
and say, "My, how you've grown."

Put it on when you play
hide-and-seek.

Then you won't have to bother looking for a place to hide.

You should probably take it off
before you kiss your grandma.

The mustache tickles.

A disguise can be handy and lots of fun...

But at the end of the day it's nice to know that you're still you.

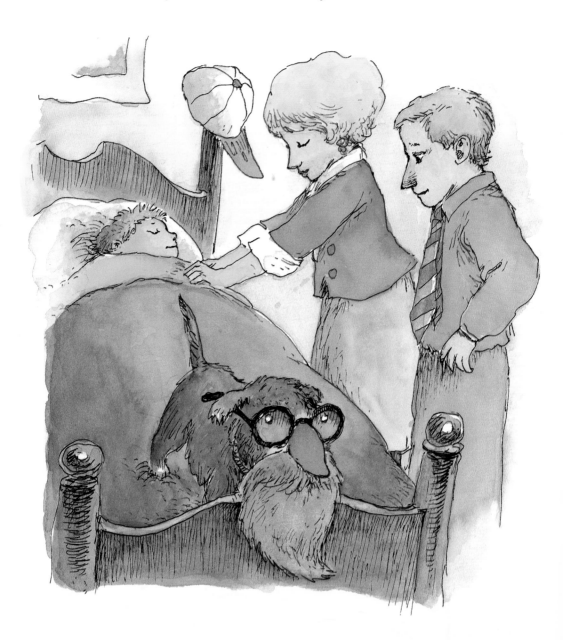